Adventures & Secret Sweet Treats

Spring At Summit Ridge Farm

Strawberry & Denver

Illustrated by
Rose Petruzzi

Volume One

Written by
Jan Prenoveau

Harwinton Public Library
Harwinton, CT

S0-ARN-549

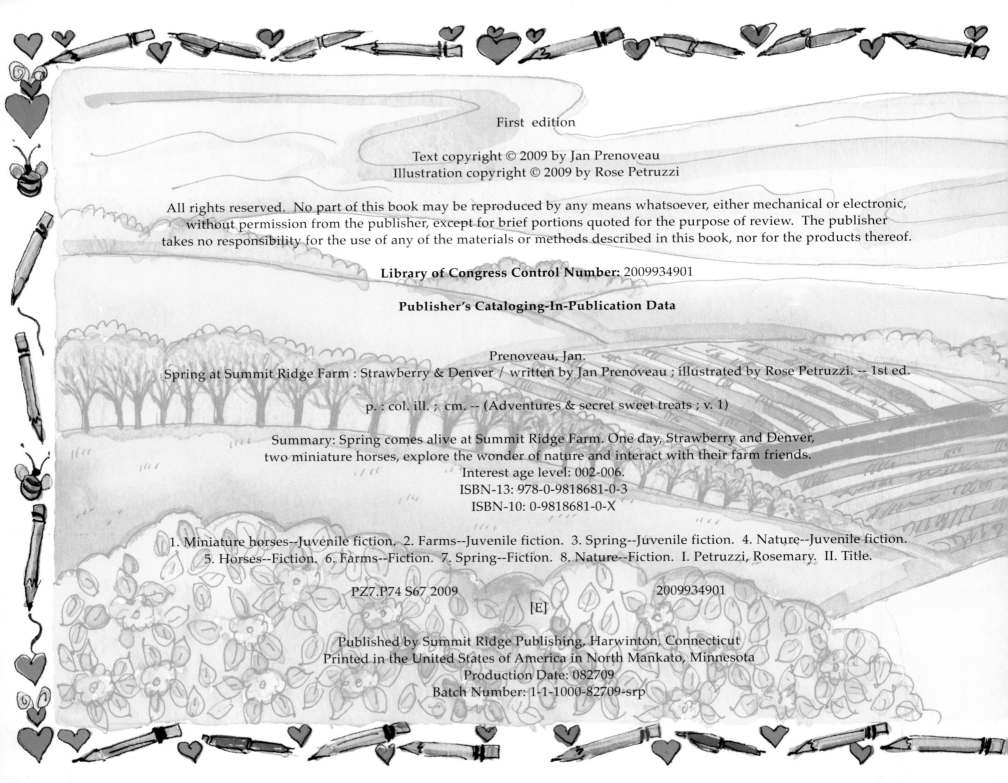

First edition

Text copyright © 2009 by Jan Prenoveau
Illustration copyright © 2009 by Rose Petruzzi

All rights reserved. No part of this book may be reproduced by any means whatsoever, either mechanical or electronic, without permission from the publisher, except for brief portions quoted for the purpose of review. The publisher takes no responsibility for the use of any of the materials or methods described in this book, nor for the products thereof.

Library of Congress Control Number: 2009934901

Publisher's Cataloging-In-Publication Data

Prenoveau, Jan.
Spring at Summit Ridge Farm : Strawberry & Denver / written by Jan Prenoveau ; illustrated by Rose Petruzzi. -- 1st ed.

p. : col. ill. ; cm. -- (Adventures & secret sweet treats ; v. 1)

Summary: Spring comes alive at Summit Ridge Farm. One day, Strawberry and Denver, two miniature horses, explore the wonder of nature and interact with their farm friends.
Interest age level: 002-006.
ISBN-13: 978-0-9818681-0-3
ISBN-10: 0-9818681-0-X

1. Miniature horses--Juvenile fiction. 2. Farms--Juvenile fiction. 3. Spring--Juvenile fiction. 4. Nature--Juvenile fiction. 5. Horses--Fiction. 6. Farms--Fiction. 7. Spring--Fiction. 8. Nature--Fiction. I. Petruzzi, Rosemary. II. Title.

PZ7.P74 S67 2009   2009934901

[E]

Published by Summit Ridge Publishing, Harwinton, Connecticut
Printed in the United States of America in North Mankato, Minnesota
Production Date: 082709
Batch Number: 1-1-1000-82709-srp

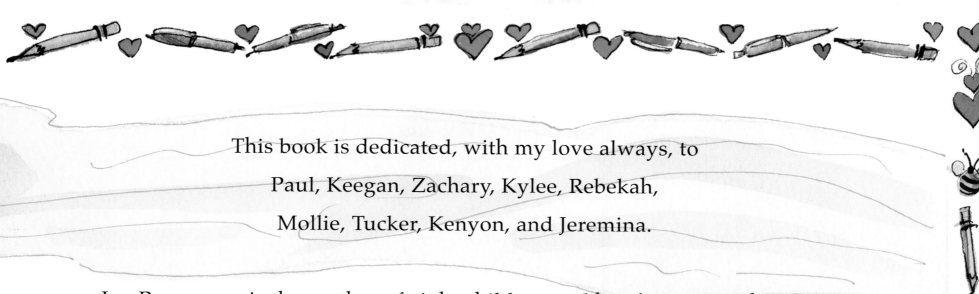

This book is dedicated, with my love always, to
Paul, Keegan, Zachary, Kylee, Rebekah,
Mollie, Tucker, Kenyon, and Jeremina.

Jan Prenoveau is the mother of eight children and has four grandchildren.
She lives in the Northwest Hills of Connecticut with her husband,
her children, and the minis. She is an avid runner and enjoys
doing road races with her family. Through her passion for
running, Jan has raised thousands of dollars for national and
international charities. Besides writing, baking, and running,
she also loves to hike and travel with her family.

It's a warm spring day at Summit Ridge Farm.
Strawberry and Denver are finishing their
breakfast, and already making plans for a
visit to their farm friends down the hill.

The crocuses and daffodils are popping their heads through
the once-frozen ground. Soon the tulips will be here.
And then the lilacs. Oh, how Strawberry and Denver
love the sweet fragrance of lilacs!

The bluebirds and robins are busy
making their nests.
Canada geese trumpet overhead,
along with the mallards, who
have found their way back to the pond.

Spring has returned
to Summit Ridge Farm.

Strawberry and Denver wonder
what has happened
to the family of turtles
who had moved in last summer.

Where have they gone so suddenly?

Dear mother hen
and her new brood
of chicks would certainly
be a wonderful sight!

12

Down the hill they trot,
through the hay fields,
past the pond,
around the apple orchard,
and on to the big gray barn.

They can't resist stopping
for a few nibbles of the new little shoots
of grass covered in misty morning dew.
Soooooo sweet!

The cows stand quietly, looking as the two little horses pass, all the while continuing to chew their cud.

The big horses nod from their paddock as
Strawberry and Denver make their way
closer to the barn.

First stop, they both agree,
will be the chicken coop.

Being "minis" has its advantages, because they are small enough to walk up the ramp, enter the henhouse door, and visit with their feathered friends.

Mother hen and baby chicks
are busy with their breakfast.

23

Strawberry and Denver help them finish up the yellow mash that lies scattered on the henhouse floor.

24

Inside the big gray barn, mother cat
meows and paces nervously
back and forth in front of a big black
abandoned tractor tire.

Mother cat remembers the minis,
and lets them pass
to have a look. What a sight!

New life has begun at Summit Ridge Farm,
as Strawberry and Denver witness
five brand-new baby kittens stirring
inside the opening of the tire.

It's getting late and is time to head back to
Strawberry's and Denver's favorite place.
The minis say their goodbyes...

...and prance back up the hill, past the chicken coop,
around the apple orchard, and past the pond...

...(where the missing family of turtles are
sunning themselves on the colorful rocks)
and up through the sweet-smelling hay fields,
to their favorite place in the entire world...

...their home in the little red barn.

Strawberry

Denver

Spring Sweet Treat

Strawberry Surprise Cupcakes

*Find this cupcake in every scene!

Here is our favorite springtime "sweet treat" for all families who enjoy baking and eating treats as much as we do!

Cupcake Ingredients:
1 Yellow Cake mix
Cupcake liners
Chocolate chips (regular size)
Miniature chocolate chips
Fresh strawberries

Buttercream Frosting Ingredients:
1 stick margarine or butter
1 tsp. vanilla extract
4 cups powdered sugar
Milk (enough for the right consistency)

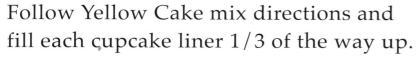

Follow Yellow Cake mix directions and
fill each cupcake liner 1/3 of the way up.

Place a "surprise" of 1/2 large strawberry
in the center of the batter in each liner.

Place 5-6 regular size chocolate chips
around the strawberry and cover
with more batter.

Enjoy our
"Strawberry Surprise Cupcakes"
especially
in the spring!

Bake according to Yellow Cake mix directions.

Cool, and then frost with buttercream frosting.

Arrange 4 strawberry halves on each cupcake
top to resemble flower petals, and fill
in each flower center with a dozen or so
miniature chocolate chips.

More About the Author...

I love baking and collecting sweet treat recipes. If you have a favorite recipe, or would like to know more about the "minis" please contact us at:

www.strawberryanddenver.com

The Family

In the spring,
eggs hatch, flowers
bloom, and the
geese come back.